Alexandra Pichard

Pen Pals

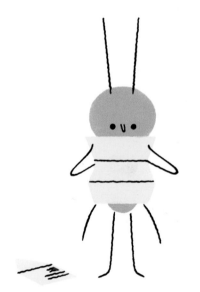

ALADDIN

New York London Toronto Sydney New Delhi

September 8th

Dear Bill,

Thank you for your letter. I think we'll get along well.

I also like to play table tennis and watch TV. My teacher says that
if our class has good grades until the end of the year, we will come
visit your school. Then we can meet!

Are you really blue? How lucky! I'm little and gray.
I have six legs. Do you have any brothers or sisters?
Do you like to play with modeling clay?

Best wishes,

Oscar

October 1st

Dear Oscar,

I don't have any brothers or sisters, but I do like modeling clay!

My cousin Olga and I played with modeling clay on Wednesday. Then we went to the Great Barrier Reef, where we found a full tube of sunscreen.

When we returned home, my stepmom made us hot chocolate and plankton beignets.

Bye,

Bill

P.S. Could you write bigger? I have bad eyesight.

October 19th

Dear Bill,

On Wednesday I couldn't play with my cousins because in the morning I had school and in the afternoon I had judo. I'm a yellow-orange belt!

It's autumn here. The wind blows hard and the leaves are red. We have to pay attention when we go outside because the leaves are falling and could hurt us. It's much less dangerous to watch TV.

What's your favorite color? I'm sending you a photo of me and my dog, Loopy. Can you send me a knickknack from your house?

Best wishes,

Oscar

November 3rd

Dear Oscar,

I put a shell and some sand from my garden in the envelope. It'll give you an idea of where I live.

What kind of dog do you have? Dachshund or golden retriever? He looks cute, but I can't see him very well in the photo.

I have a goldfish named Goliath.

My favorite colors are 1) blue, 2) purple, 3) yellow. What's yours?

Until later,

Bill

November 18th

Dear Bill,

Thank you for the hat!

My favorite color is blue, like you, then purple, and lastly yellow.

It's true that my dog is very cute. He's a Labrador. Or a dachshund. I don't know anymore.

I have a gift for you too: they are knitted mittens from my mom! Do you like them? It's starting to get cold and I thought they would make you happy.

Did you make a Christmas list?

Best wishes,

Oscar

December 5th

Dear Oscar,

The mittens are super! I put them on every day.
Too bad that there were only six!

As thanks, I'm sending the full tube of sunscreen
I found last October. It'll be more useful to you
than it is to me.

For Christmas I asked for a 2D console,
Super Marco, Marco 4, a vampire costume,
Tintin and the Mysterious Island of Rhé, and
some glow-in-the-dark table tennis balls.

What did you ask for from Santa Claus?

Until next time,

Bill

December 25th

Dear Bill,

Today I had a great day . . . naturally, since it's Christmas!

I got a robot figurine that can transform into a truck and retransform into a robot!

I also got the last book about the adventures of Jack the Tarantula. Have you read it? I'm sending you the first three books. Let me know if you like them!

Best wishes,

Oscar

P.S. The class average is 14.5/20. That means we can visit in June!

Dear Oscar,

December

Dear Bill,

January 16th

Dear Oscar,

I can't wait for you to come! To stay busy until then, I play Super Marco every day. I'm already on level seven of world five.

Thank you for Jack the Tarantula. I really loved it! In exchange, I'm giving you my favorite sea-lion-wool socks. They're yours, so take care of them.

Bye,

Bill

February 10th

Dear Bill,

I'll take care of your socks like they're the apple of my eye. I promise.

Today it was Mardi Gras. My dad and I made crepe batter. Then we cooked the crepes and flipped them in the pan. It was so fun! And so delicious! I hope you like apricot jam because I put some in the crepe I sent.

Have you ever had the hiccups?

Best wishes,

Oscar

March 8th

Dear Oscar,

One day I had the hiccups. To stop them I brushed my teeth, and it worked! What about you?

Have you ever played cup-and-ball?

Thank you for the crepe. I loved it! Since I don't know how to cook, I wanted to make you a drawing. You can frame it, or hang it directly on your bedroom wall.

High-eight,

Bill

April 4th

Dear Bill,

So talented! I hung your drawing above my bed between the posters of Mimi King and Rick Holiday, my favorite singers.

I was playing in the garden with my dog, Loopy, when I found a four-leaf clover. Take it, and it will bring you happiness!

By the way, have you finished Super Marco?

Best wishes,

Oscar

May 6th

Dear Oscar,

I beat the last monster, a two-headed leech. I can finally dedicate myself to my passion: the TV!

Thank you for the clover! I'm sending you a starfish with four arms. Put it in your pocket and it'll bring you luck!

Bye-bye,

Bill

June 10th

Dear Bill,

Catastrophe! This morning our teacher broke three legs and her antennae in gym class. Now the class trip to the sea is canceled! I am disappointed, upset, and crushed!

Best wishes,

Oscar

June 19th

Dear Oscar,

Don't panic! I'm preparing a package for you that will raise your spirits. I can't say any more about it yet. . . .

See you soon,

Bill

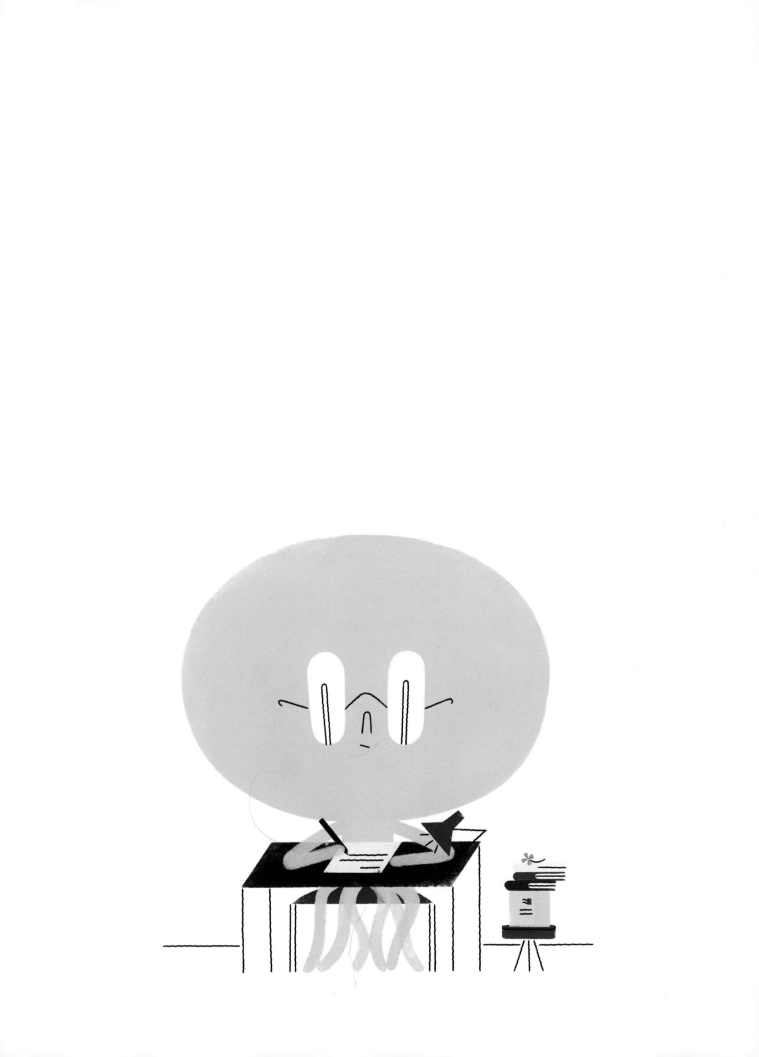

OSCAR

ALADDIN

An imprint of Simon & Schuster
Children's Publishing Division

1230 Avenue of the Americas
New York, New York 10020

First Aladdin hardcover edition January 2017

Copyright © 2014 by Gallimard Jeunesse

Published by arrangement with Gallimard Jeunesse

English language translation copyright © 2017
by Simon & Schuster, Inc.

Originally published in France in 2014 as *Cher Bill*
by Gallimard Jeunesse

For information about special discounts for bulk purchases,
please contact Simon & Schuster Special Sales at
1-866-506-1949 or business@simonandschuster.com.

The Simon & Schuster Speakers Bureau can bring authors
to your live event. For more information or to book an
event contact the Simon & Schuster Speakers Bureau
at 1-866-248-3049 or visit our website at
www.simonspeakers.com.

Designed by Steve Scott

The text of this book was set in
Sassoon Primary.

Manufactured in China 1016 SCP

2 4 6 8 10 9 7 5 3 1

Library of Congress Control Number: 2016948702

ISBN 978-1-4814-7247-0 (hc)

ISBN 978-1-4814-7248-7 (eBook)